BERT

The Fairies' Fashion Expert

For Moira Stansfield
J. W.

For the Paul Family, Klub Barbounia members
K. P.

ORCHARD BOOKS
338 Euston Road, London NW1 3BH
Orchard Books Australia
Level 17/207 Kent Street, Sydney, NSW 2000
ISBN 1 84362 149 5 (paperback)
First published in Great Britain in 2004
First paperback publication in 2005
Text © Jeanne Willis 2004
Illustrations © Korky Paul 2004
The rights of Jeanne Willis to be identified as the author
and of Korky Paul to be identified as the illustrator of this
work have been asserted by them in accordance with the
Copyright, Designs and Patents Act, 1988.
A CIP catalogue record for this book is available
from the British Library.
1 3 5 7 9 10 8 6 4 2 (paperback)
Printed and bound in China
Orchard Books is a division of Hachette Children's Books

BERT

The Fairies' Fashion Expert

Jeanne Willis * Korky Paul

ORCHARD BOOKS

BERT

The Fairies' Fashion Expert

Hello, darlings, my name's Bert.
Excuse me while I sew this shirt,
It's one I've recently designed.
Is that the time? I'm all behind!

I've been stitching frocks all night,
They're on that hanger to your right.
Look very hard - they're rather small.
I made them for the Pixie Ball.

All the fairies come to me,
I am their Fashion Expert, see?
I make designer clothes for all
The magic folk - I'm big on small.

Snow White's a customer of mine,
A smashing girl. Her hair's divine!
She's been coming here for years.
I dress her dwarfs, the little dears.

I made this gorgeous hat for Doc,
And here is little Dopey's smock
With buttons that do up themselves
(I had them magicked by some elves).

Here's Sneezy's coat. Would you believe
He always wipes it on his sleeve?
That's why I've sewn a panel there
In sneeze-proof fabric, easy-care.

Fashion is a funny game.

I had this client – what's his name?

Oh, Rumpelstiltskin. That was it.

I shouldn't say, but what a twit!

He comes in with a load of straw
And dumps it there, right on my floor.
"Now spin it into gold!" he screams.
"Get stuffed!" I told him. "In your dreams."

"Gold's so yesterday," I said,
"I'll make you something fab in red
With spots on. It would match your face!"
He stamped his foot and left the place.

PIXIES

FAIRIES

GOBLINS

Cinderella's been here twice.

Her wedding gown was really nice.

Her God-Ma picked those ghastly shoes.

(Glass isn't something I would choose.)

There's the phone! I'm on my knees!
"Bert's Fashion . . . who is calling please?"
Oh, sugar plums! It's the Wicked Fairy!
Bolt the doors, she's really scary!

She wants a special magic cloak,
I'd rather swallow pins and choke!
She poisons innocent princesses,
And I hate the way she dresses.

I'll hide - I'm under my machine!
(A...tchoo! This carpet needs a clean.)
The fairy's coming! I can tell
By her rotten Eau-de-Cabbage smell.

That big, bad fairy's in my shop.
She's seen me! Eek! I'm for the chop!
She hisses, "Glad that we could meet -
Do stop grovelling at my feet!"

So up I get and take her coat.
(Pooh! It's stinky as a stoat!)
I draw designs and pour the tea
And this is what she says to me:

"Make my cloak from Tortoise Silk
Washed in silver Seahorse Milk,
Trimmed with Dragon's Eggs in gold
And lined with Shark's Fur, icy cold.

"I'll pick it up tomorrow noon."
(Excuse me? That is far too soon!)
"If it's not ready, Bert," she grins,
"I'll curse your needles and your pins."

The fashion world knows I'm the best,
I've got Fairyland all dressed.
But even with my natural flair
I can't make magic cloaks from air.

I've got fabric by the ton
But none of it is tortoise-spun.
Nor washed in Seahorse Milk, I fear . . .
There is no call for it round here.

Dragon's Eggs just come in blue,
Not gold! Whatever shall I do?
As for Shark's Fur, what a twit!
I know the sharks won't part with it.

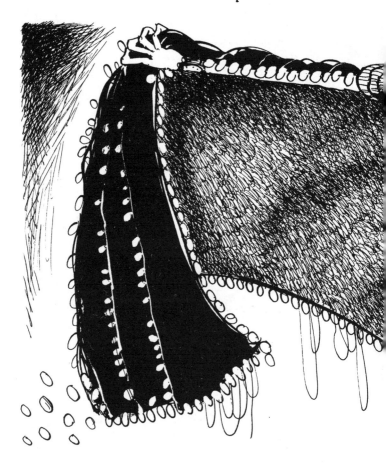

I've cut some corners - here's the cloak,
It's hardly magic. What a joke!
It's man-made silk. The fur's not real,
It's cheap old nylon stuff - you feel!

The eggs? They only came from hens.
I coloured in the shells with pens.
Oh well, it's fashionable. It's fun!
(Unless it rains and the felt-tips run.)

That fairy should be here - she's late!
Perhaps I muddled up the date?
I'll check in my appointment book.
Uh-oh! She's parked her broomstick, look!

She looks quite fierce, I have to say,
I really wish she'd go away.
I'm scared she'll cast a wicked spell -
She's coming! Sell it, Bertie, sell!

"Good morning, Madam! Oooh, I say,
Your hair looks marvellous today."
She scowls and gives my ribs a poke.
"Oh, shut up, Bertie. Where's my cloak?"

"The finest Tortoise Silk!" I cry.
"The softest Shark's Fur too," I lie,
"With Dragon's Eggs, they're very rare –
It suits you perfectly, I swear!"

"But is it magic?" she remarks.
"Is the lining really Shark's?
If it's true and all is well,
You'll be a frog when I try this spell."

She curses me and waves her wand.
"Turn green!" she screams. " Hop in a pond!"
The spell won't work. "There's some mistake,"
She cries, "which means this cloak is fake!"

"Curse your thread and curse your needles
And your sequins, Bert!" she wheedles.
"Skirts will swivel! Trousers split!
Shirts and jackets will not fit!"

40

"Madam wishes to complain?
Please take a seat. Let me explain..."
But OUCH! She sits upon a pin!
(I put it there - it sticks right in!)

"I'm weary, I must close my eyes
And sleep for a hundred years," she sighs.
"That wretched pin was cursed!" she snores.
"Is Sleeping Beauty a client of yours?"

"Indeed she is! She lent the pin
In case the likes of you came in!
I've pricked you, just like you pricked her.
History repeating itself, as it were!"

Back to business! Do you see
Why fairy folk won't mess with me?
So don't muck about if you need a suit...
I might turn you into a big, fat newt!

Written by Jeanne Willis ✳ Illustrated by Korky Paul

All priced at £3.99 each

Crazy Jobs are available from all good book shops, or can be ordered direct
from the publisher: Orchard Books, PO BOX 29, Douglas IM99 1BQ
Credit card orders please telephone 01624 836000
or fax 01624 837033 or visit our Internet site: www.wattspub.co.uk
or e-mail: bookshop@enterprise.net for details.

To order please quote title, author and ISBN
and your full name and address.
Cheques and postal orders should be made payable to 'Bookpost plc.'
Postage and packing is FREE within the UK
(overseas customers should add £1.00 per book).
Prices and availability are subject to change.